ALFIE AND the DRAGON

www.alfieandthedragon.com

redstart

First published in the United Kingdom by Redstart Publishing
www.redstartpublishing.com

ISBN 978-0-9934904-0-8
Printed in the UK
First printed December 2015
Second edition printed October 2017

Written by Tony Roberts
Illustrated by Lauren Jones - www.phantascope.net
Designed by Aron Owen - www.aronowen.com

Dragons are real... aren't they?

There are lots of stories and legends about dragons but has anyone ever seen a real, live, fire breathing, people chomping, earth scorching dragon?

Probably not.

Alfie *loves* dragons.

He often lies in bed at night imagining there are dragons living in faraway lands, flying high through the air, breathing great jets of fire and sitting on piles of treasure in glittering caves deep under the mountains.

He would dream about riding a dragon, up into the sky, far away over the towering jagged mountains to the enchanted and ancient country of Wales - Where the dragons live.

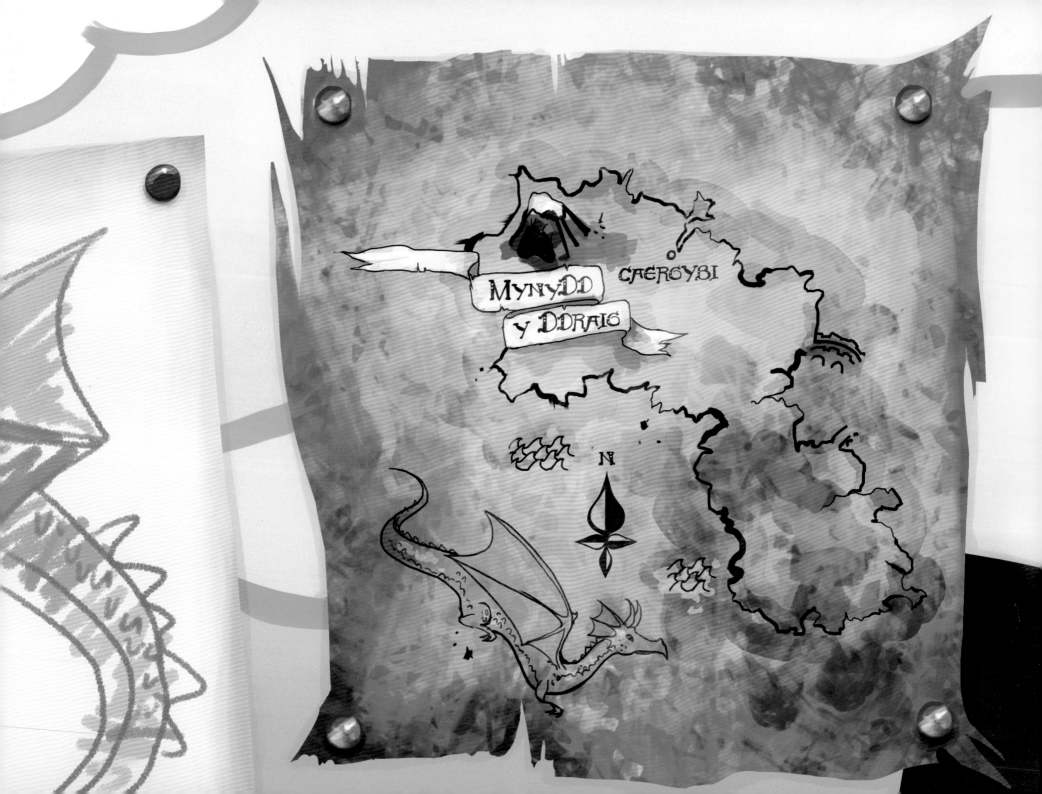

Alfie's uncle lives in Wales.
Wales is an ancient land full of magic and legend.

During his summer holidays, Alfie loves to stay with his uncle,
who lives in a very beautiful place, with a mysterious Welsh name... Caergybi.

"Cair-gu-bee," Alfie would whisper to himself over and over again.

Every night at bed time, Alfie's uncle would tell him wonderful stories of the dragons that lived in the *old, old* caves of Fire Mountain in Caergybi.

"How do I speak to dragons?" asked Alfie.

"Welsh is the official language of dragons, so you have to speak Welsh to the dragons of Fire Mountain," said his uncle.

"Say Fire Mountain in Welsh Alfie... *Mynydd Tân!*" roared his uncle.

"Mun-ith taan!" shouted Alfie.

"Excellent Alfie... excellent," exclaimed his uncle.

Late one warm summer's evening just before bed time, Alfie pleaded with his uncle to tell him more about the dragons of Fire Mountain.

"Not now I'm afraid it's far too late, it's time for bed young Alfie!" said his uncle, who made Alfie squeal with laughter, by tickling him and shouting;

"Hide Alfie...
the dragon's coming!"...

"The dragon's coming!"

shouted Alfie back to his uncle, laughing very loudly,
whilst quickly diving under the covers of his bed.

Alfie's uncle tucked him in tight and said,
"Remember Alfie, if you ever want to talk to dragons,
you must speak these magic Welsh words...

Mynydd Tân!"

"Mun-ith taan, Mun-ith taan,"
Alfie whispered to himself as he slipped gently off to sleep.

It was very late at night,
or very early in the morning... depending on how you look at it.

Alfie yawned, stretched his arms, rolled over and fell out of bed...

Bump.
He hit the floor.

"Ow!"
He rubbed his head... now he was wide awake.

He heard a strange noise coming from the back of the house.
Alfie crept carefully over to his bedroom window
and gazed up into the night sky.

The sky was very dark.
The stars were shining bright.

But, one star was shining brighter than all of the rest,
and it was moving swiftly across the sky.

Alfie rubbed his eyes and stared out of the window.

The star was getting bigger and bigger,
and it was coming rapidly towards him.

Alfie's heart pounded in his chest.
He thought of running back to bed and hiding under the covers,
but - he didn't.

He tiptoed quietly down the stairs,
creeping along the hall, slowly
turned the key in the back door
and stepped carefully outside.

The night was very dark and Alfie
was *so scared*, but do you know -
he didn't run back into the house.

He kept going. Through the little gate, past the dark dark bushes and into the garden.

Alfie stood in the middle of the garden and stared up into the sky.

Whoosh whoosh

came a sound from above, like a fierce wind rushing through the trees.

Alfie dived under the hedge and did not dare to move.

The whooshing sound got louder and louder then suddenly...

Thump.

The ground shuddered.
Alfie's heart was pounding so hard he thought it would burst out of his chest.

There was an eerie silence and then Alfie heard a strange snuffling and shuffling sound.
He peeked out through his fingers, hardly daring to look.

What do you think he saw?

A *huge* scaly foot was squashing his uncle's flowers flat.
Alfie opened his fingers a little bit more and stared out into the night, hardly daring to breathe.
Attached to the huge scaly foot was a huge scaly leg and an *enormous* golden body.

Can you guess what Alfie saw next?...

The majestic golden head of a dragon, which was crowned with
fabulous golden horns.

Alfie buried his face in his trembling hands.

There was more snuffling and shuffling and a strange clinking sound,
like the jangling of a thousand coins in a sack full of glittering treasure.

He felt hot steamy breath on his face and a strange smell of...
Bananas.

Alfie carefully peeked through his fingers again.

Do you know what he saw?...

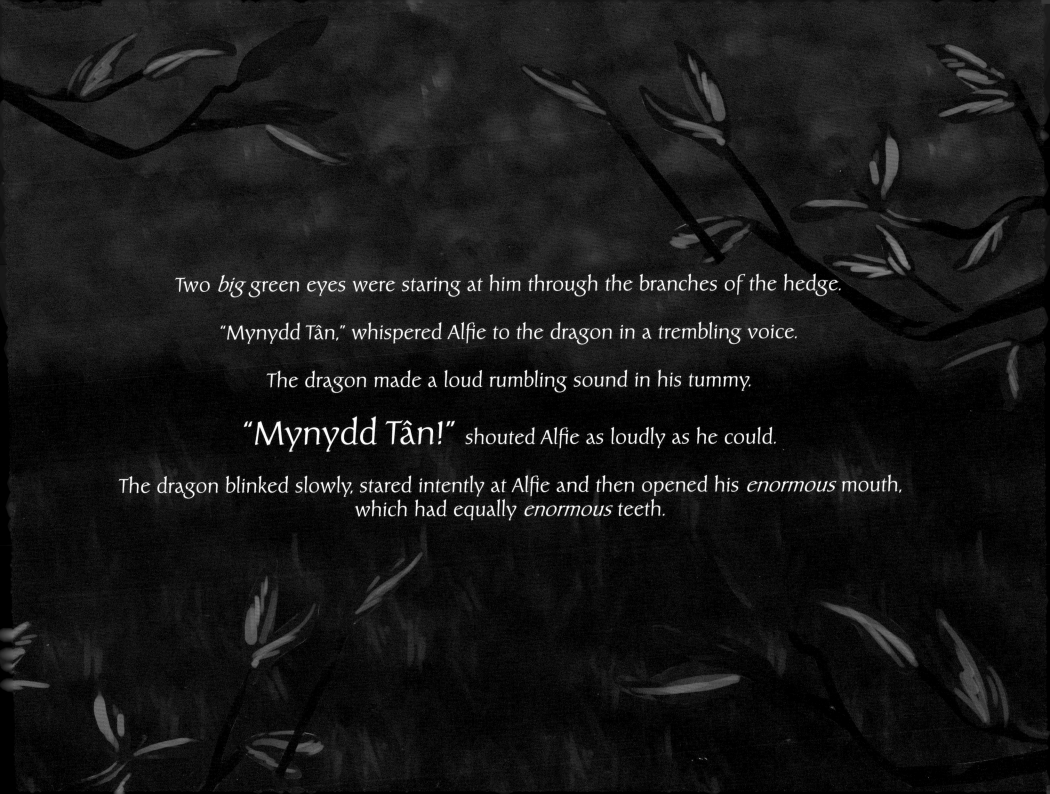

Two *big* green eyes were staring at him through the branches of the hedge.

"Mynydd Tân," whispered Alfie to the dragon in a trembling voice.

The dragon made a loud rumbling sound in his tummy.

"Mynydd Tân!" shouted Alfie as loudly as he could.

The dragon blinked slowly, stared intently at Alfie and then opened his *enormous* mouth, which had equally *enormous* teeth.

Hmmmmmm-rrrrrrraughghgh,

came a low rolling sound from the dragon's throat.

"Mynydd Tân!... *hmmmmmm!*

You must be Alfie!" said the dragon in the deepest,
most beautiful voice Alfie had ever heard.

"You're a *real...* d-d-dragon," stuttered Alfie in a trembling voice.
"H-H-How do you know my name?"

"Dragons know many things young master, now come out
from under that hedge!" he boomed.

Alfie slowly crawled out and looked up.
The dragon was *huge* and had the most beautiful golden
scales all the way from the tip of his tail to his glistening
golden head.

"Wow!" gasped Alfie, "you're *magnificent!*"

"Do you really think so?" said the dragon (who was obviously pleased).
"Apart from this," he said, patting his tummy,
"too many banana pancakes.
Mmmmm... they're my favourite."

"That's why you smell of bananas!" exclaimed Alfie,
forgetting he was speaking to an enormous and powerful dragon.

"Do I really?" said the dragon, who did not seem angry at all.
"Oh dear I must brush my teeth more."

"Alfie, my name is Meredydd, Son of Idris the Golden and
I live under the mountain of Caergybi.
I name you, Alfie, dragon friend!"

"*Dragon friend,*" whispered Alfie. "You mean we could really be friends?"
"Of course," said the dragon, "and friends share secrets.

Now then, let's go for a ride!"

Alfie could hardly believe his ears. He was *really* going to ride on a dragon.
The dragon bent his huge front leg and said, "climb up Alfie."
He climbed up the golden leg, over the shiny gleaming scales and onto the dragon's back.

"Are you ready!" boomed the dragon.

"Oh yes!" shouted Alfie.

The dragon opened his fantastic wings and rose into the sky.

"Woohooooooooooo!"
shouted Alfie over the noise of the rushing wind.

They rose *up* into the sky, towards the twinkling stars.
Higher and higher they rose.

"Hold on tight Alfie!" roared the dragon.

"We're going to fly past my cave and over the mountain."

Higher and higher they went up into the night sky until suddenly the dragon folded back his magnificent wings and dived headlong towards the sea. They were going *so fast*, that Alfie's tummy turned upside down and inside out.

He could see Fire Mountain ahead and the shining sea below. The dragon swooped low over the waves and roared, "Look Alfie, there's my cave!"

Alfie could see a dark opening in the rock, just above the foam capped waves. It was hidden below a big white foghorn which was perched on a very high cliff towering over the sea.

"I can see it!" shouted Alfie.

The dragon then raced across the water, around a lighthouse and climbed high into the air once more.

Alfie could see the whole of Fire Mountain and the mountains of Wales in the distance.

The Dragon began to glide through the darkness towards the ground below.

"Time to go home now young Alfie!" said the dragon, as he beat his powerful wings, gracefully swooping over the town and down through the valleys.

"Wooooohooooo!" shouted Alfie once more.

He heard a low rumbling sound... the dragon was laughing.

Steadily and slowly he descended, skimming rooftops and chimney stacks until Alfie could see the familiar lights of his uncle's house in the distance. The dragon slowed down and swooped gracefully back into the garden.

Thump, he landed... right in the flower bed.

"Climb down Alfie," said the dragon.

Alfie slid down the glistening scales and over the dragons leg, safely on to the grass.

"Thank you! Thank you!" said Alfie excitedly.
"You are the *nicest*, most wonderful dragon *ever*.
Will I ever see you again?"

"Of course you will Alfie," said the dragon.

"I have a secret signal. When I am coming, I will breathe my fiery breath onto the sea
to make a great fog, and the foghorn will blow."

The dragon took a deep breath and made the sound of a foghorn...

"Mwahhhhhooooooahh!

When you hear this sound, come to the garden and I will be here waiting for you.
Until then, goodbye young Alfie, dragon friend."

Alfie watched wondrously as the dragon leapt into the air, unfurled his wings and raced off into the distance.

Hardly daring to believe what had just happened Alfie crept quietly back into the house, tiptoed up the stairs and slipped into bed.

"Alfie, *dragon friend*," he whispered to himself over and over again until he fell fast asleep.

Can you guess what he dreamt about?

Of course... dragons!

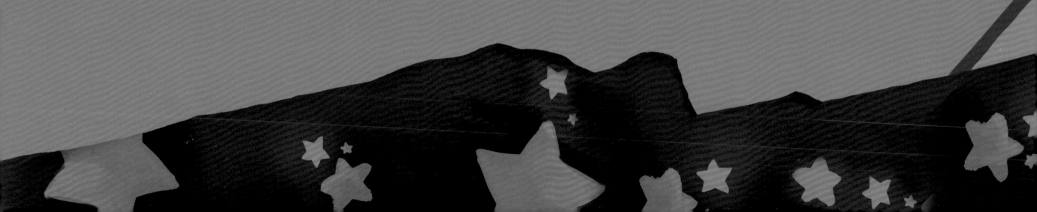

The next morning Alfie woke to the wonderful smell of bacon and sausages.

He jumped out of bed and ran downstairs excitedly.

"Uncle! Uncle! Dragons are *real!*" he gasped.

"I met one last night and his name was Meredydd.
He took me *flying* past his cave up into the sky and over the mountain!"

"Dragons... *real?*" said his uncle

"Of course they are Alfie...
of course they are."

If you ever happen to be in deepest, darkest Wales, then be sure to visit Fire Mountain, in the ancient town of Caergybi. Look up into the night, if you see a bright star, or a fiery dot zooming across the sky, it might be...

Alfie's dragon.

The End

Upcoming books:
Alfie's Dragon and the Banana Crystals
Millie's Magical Wellies
Where's My Guinea Pig?

These books and more will be available from:
www.redstartpublishing.com